Linda The Loser

By Sarah Lynn Shade

Dedicated to my parents, Dale and Brenda Shade, who personally experienced a Divine betrothal.

ISBN# 0-9788703-3-6

All Scripture quotations are taken from the Holy Bible, King James Version

This is a work of fiction. Names, characters, and plot line are products of the author's imagination. Any resemblance to real people, living or dead, is purely coincidental.

Printed By:

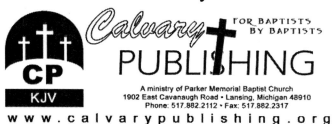

FOR BAPTISTS
BY BAPTISTS

A ministry of Parker Memorial Baptist Church
1902 East Cavanaugh Road • Lansing, Michigan 48910
Phone: 517.882.2112 • Fax: 517.882.2317
w w w . c a l v a r y p u b l i s h i n g . o r g

For additional copies visit:
www.localchurchbiblepublishers.com

Also available in the Divine Betrothal Series

Bethany's Betrothal $5.00

Bethany Olsen, age twenty-two, desires nothing more than to be happily married. After having faced three heartbreaks, things aren't looking so good. Realizing she can no longer endure the pain of rejection, Bethany promptly turns her back on courtship and leaves the choice of her mate entirely up to God. Not until she truly learns to put her full faith and trust in God, is Bethany granted the Divine betrothal she has been prayerfully seeking.

Mandy and the Mix Up $5.00

Mandy Dixon is already twenty-six and still not spoken for. Her only option in sight is her life-long friend, Clyde Anderson, but Clyde advises her to wait for God's perfect choice. Mandy wants to trust her friend's counsel, but who ever heard of Divine betrothal? And did God really have someone special picked out for her from the time she was born? Mandy's about to find out that a mix-up in her past may hold the key to her future.

Acknowledgements

First of all, I would like to thank God for giving me the desire to become an author, and for His guidance throughout the writing of this second book in the Divine Betrothal Series.

Second, I would like to thank everyone involved with Local Church Bible Publishers, and Calvary Publishing for making the publication of this book possible. Many thanks to Mark Chartier for his time and effort throughout the entire process. Also, thanks is due to all the editors and proof-readers for their help, suggestions, and support.

Special thanks to Santiago Lopez for his cover design, Crystall Bridger for her photography, and John and Nina Vesel for the use of their wedding rings.

Table of Contents

Chapter One

A Rainy Day

September rain pelted the second story window of Lennard's Christian Bookstore. The sidewalk down below had transformed into a shallow stream, battered with the steady onslaught of pouring raindrops. Occasionally, a man or a woman would bustle by, clutching their umbrellas as temporary solitude from the unmerciful downpour. But Linda Lennard barely noticed as she stared aimlessly out the window. About ten minutes ago, she had curled up on the window seat, dust rag forgotten, as her thoughts drifted miles away.

Unlike the present weather, Linda's memories took her to a warm, sunny afternoon in August. It was seven years ago on a Sunday, and the members of Courtland Baptist Church were having a going-away party for a young man named Michael Donavan. Linda, just sixteen at the time, was very fond of this eighteen-year-old boy. He wasn't like the other boys in the church—senseless, foolish, and self-centered. He had a sober outlook on life and wanted nothing more than to amount to something for God.

Linda had always respected him in a way she found impossible with other young men her age. Not that she had ever let on to him that she liked him, but she had always held on to the secret hope that one day he would find her as admirable as she did him.

As she served up glasses of sweet punch, she stared at him across the grassy churchyard as he conversed with friends and family. All were happily congratulating him on his recent success and wishing him well in his next chapter in life. In less than a week, Michael would be gone, embracing the life of a college student. Linda could hardly bear the thought. A whole year without him? If only she had the nerve to tell him how she really felt.

Suddenly, Michael disengaged from his present conversation and began strolling across the yard toward the table Linda stood at. Immediately, she felt her pulse quicken. Her face flushed red, her palms grew sweaty, and her throat constricted, causing what she knew could become a hindrance if she were forced to speak. Her eyes lowered as Michael approached the serving table.

"Hi, Linda," he said, casually. "Well, I guess it's goodbye, actually," he added with a chuckle. Linda looked up into his blue eyes. They bore a sparkle of excitement. He was looking forward to leaving.

"I'm going to miss everyone here, but I can't wait to see what takes place in these next few years," Michael continued, helping himself to a glass of punch. "I mean, what if God calls me to preach while I'm studying the Bible?"

"What if He doesn't?" Linda asked a little too abruptly.

Michael's expression changed to that of a thoughtful frown. "Well," he said, "I'm open to anything really. I want God to use me in whatever way He sees fit. I may come back from college and become a preacher, an assistant pastor, a Sunday School teacher, or just a faithful Christian who knows his Bible!" He grinned exuberantly.

"How many years will you be going for?" Linda asked, swallowing hard.

"Oh, four or five. I'm not sure yet," Michael answered, brushing a fly off his short, brown hair.

"Don't you think that's...well...a long time to be away?" Linda asked, her heart racing.

"It's not that long," Michael replied, shrugging his shoulders. "Besides, I'll be back for the summer each year. It'll go by fast."

Maybe for you, Linda thought.

"Well, I guess I'll be seeing you around," Michael told her. "Next summer," he added with a nod.

Wait! I don't want you to leave! Linda wanted to say. *I can't bear the thought of not seeing you for a whole year. You're different than the other boys, and...and I like you! What will I do without you, Michael?*

Linda had so much she wanted to say, but couldn't. Michael was eighteen. He had made his plans for the future. She was only sixteen. He probably saw her as a child. It was highly unlikely he shared the same feelings for her as she had for him. Oh, well. Maybe by next summer she would have enough courage to tell him her heart.

But Linda never had that chance. As Michael stepped away from the table and rejoined the milling crowd, she knew it was the last time she would get to talk to him for a whole year, but little did she know, it would be much longer than that. Shortly after Michael's departure for college, his family moved out of state. He would be visiting for the summer, but not in Pennsylvania.

Over and over and over, Linda replayed that scene in her mind. It had now been seven years since she had seen or heard from him. Sometimes she changed the scene and imagined herself saying things she wished she had said.

"Hi, Linda. Well, I guess it's goodbye, actually."

"Yeah," Linda imagined herself saying. "It will seem weird not having you around."

"I know. I'm going to miss everyone here, but I can't wait to see what takes place in these next few years. I mean, what if God calls me to preach while I'm studying the Bible?"

"That would be great!" Linda said. She wished she had really been that supportive at the time. Maybe it would have meant something to Michael. "Even if you only end up an assistant pastor, or a Sunday

School teacher, or just a faithful Christian, I'm sure God will use you in a mighty way."

"Thanks, Linda. You're a real encouragement. I won't soon forget you. You've always been a special person in my life."

Linda's heart leaped as she smiled up at Michael. He wouldn't soon forget her. She'd always been a special person in his life. Suddenly, a year didn't seem that long. Why, it was only…

"Linda."

The cloud of warm feelings and sunshine slowly melted away and was replaced by the soft, steady rhythm of falling rain. Reality had returned, and with it, the unpleasant fact that Linda had never really been able to say what she had wanted to say to Michael.

"Linda, there are things that still need to be done," Mr. Lennard said. "Have you finished dusting the shelves yet?"

Linda sighed and looked down at the dust rag lying beside her on the window seat. "Not yet," she answered.

"This kind of weather keeps people indoors mostly," Mr. Lennard noted, staring down at the wet streets. "We should take advantage of the slow business and get some work done this afternoon."

"All right," Linda agreed. She slowly stood up and stretched; then scanned the long shelves of books that lined both walls on either side of the window. More shelves stood in neat rows across the middle of the large room, and still more lined the other walls.

Mr. Lennard's two-story bookstore was a lot of work for just two people to maintain. During the summer months, Linda's mother and six siblings would often be called on to help, but now school had begun, and Mrs. Lennard's home schooling had taken priority. Linda had graduated five years ago, and had joined her father in the long, busy days of running the bookstore. Linda's sister, Amy, was almost eighteen and had only one year of school left. Amy loved books and could not wait for the day when she would be recruited to full-time work in the bookstore. Stephen was fifteen and a freshman in high school. He could be a lot of help when it came to lifting heavy boxes of books, but he preferred spending his days tending to the family farm. Esther was in seventh grade, Jane was in fourth grade, and Jonah and Micah were in first grade. The Lennard household was a happy one, but the family had their work cut out for them.

Everyone shared a part, but between helping in the bookstore, doing farm chores, carrying out certain household duties, and caring for her younger siblings, Linda felt she most certainly carried the bulk of the load. Often, she would spend the long, monotonous hours of work, imagining herself in more interesting settings. Sometimes she imagined herself married, or away at college like some of her friends. At times, she would even pretend she was a poor, mistreated, captive slave. The work was still there, but at least she could dream that one day a handsome young man would come along and rescue her from her cruel and unmerciful master.

About half an hour later, Linda had finally finished the dusting and was busy cleaning the upper story front window when she saw a blue car pull up down below. She temporarily stopped wiping the glass and watched as three of her church friends climbed out of the car. Laughing and talking among themselves, the three girls headed toward the front door.

Linda dropped the rag and turned to face her father who was unpacking his last box from the recent shipment. "Dad, my friends are here," she told him. "I'll go down and see what they want."

Linda heard the bell above the door jingle as she hurried downstairs.

"Hi, Linda," Becky said, hurrying in out of the rain. Becky was twenty years old and already owned her own seamstress shop with a little apartment above it. "I can't believe all the rain," she whimpered, smoothing her silky, red hair.

"Oh, it's not that bad," twenty-two-year-old Jessica proclaimed. "I'm sure it'll let up soon." Jessica was an accomplished pianist who had taken music lessons as a child and had then gone on to study music in college where she received a master's degree. She was blond, beautiful, and very professional.

"So, Linda. Are you busy right now?"

Linda turned to face the eldest of the trio. At twenty-three, Cathy was the same age as Linda and probably had the most in common with her. She had her own apartment and held a waitressing job at the local family restaurant. She had shoulder-length, dark curls, and a soft smile.

"Well, other than helping out here at the bookstore, I don't have any plans, if that's what you mean," Linda answered.

"We were just on our way to the mall, and thought we'd stop by and see if you wanted to come along," Becky told her.

"Really?" Linda's face lit up. "That sounds like fun! Let me go ask my dad. I'll be right back."

Racing up the stairs, Linda found her father stacking empty boxes in the second-floor storage room.

"Dad, my friends, Cathy, Becky, and Jessica, want to know if I can ride along to the mall with them. Please say yes! I've finished the dusting, and all the front windows have been washed," Linda spilled out in one breath. "I promise I'll be home by whatever time you wish. Please say I can go!"

Mr. Lennard sighed and turned to face his oldest daughter. His brown eyes looked tired and almost sad, but Linda hoped maybe he could find it in his heart to tell her that he would manage without her for the rest of the afternoon.

"Linda," Mr. Lennard began. "You know how I feel about you running off by yourself to places like that."

"But I won't be alone," Linda assured him. "I'll be with three friends."

"Well, you know what I mean," her father replied. "Besides, I'm sure your mother is going to need your help after a long day with the children." Linda's face fell as he continued. "I'll be closing in a couple hours, and you know how your mother would feel if I came home without you. I'm sorry, but you will have to tell them 'no'."

Linda turned and walked back downstairs, blushing with embarrassment. Why did her father have to treat her like such a child? It was so humiliating.

"I can't go," she said simply.

"Oh, why not?" Jessica cried. "We can have you back by a certain time."

"No, I...I have things I have to do," Linda insisted. "I just can't come."

"But you always have things to do. Can't you take a break once in a while?" Becky prompted.

"Don't push her," Cathy interrupted. "Linda, we all know it's your overly-strict father. He never lets you do anything. You're twenty-three, and he treats you like an adolescent."

"He...he has his reasons," Linda mumbled, although she herself wasn't quite sure what those reasons were.

"Well, if he ever decides to lighten up on the reins, let us know," Jessica said, as the three girls headed for the door.

Linda watched out the front window as her three friends re-entered the car and sped down the wet street, leaving her in the dust once again. Linda Lennard--the captive slave.

Chapter Two

Farm Girl

Linda's heart sank lower and lower as she stared out the front window and envisioned all the fun she could have had if her father had only granted her request. Why was he always so protective? It wasn't like this was the first time. Cathy, Becky, Jessica, and Linda had grown up together. They had gone to the same church for years, and yet Linda had always seemed to be one step behind.

Cathy, Becky, and Jessica had all acquired their driver's permits right at sixteen, whereas Linda had been made to wait until her twenty-first birthday. Linda had watched as each one of her friends graduated high school and then went on to pursue their chosen careers. Mr. Lennard firmly believed that a young lady's place was to remain in her home until the day she married, so college or career was never an option for Linda.

A few years ago, she had asked, "What will become of me if I never get married?"

"Then perhaps God will reveal a different plan for your life," Mr. Lennard had replied. "Until then, you can serve Him just fine right where you are."

Linda watched as the rain finally tapered off, and the sun began to push its way out from behind the clouds. She sighed as she turned from the window and faced the little mirror hanging by the cash register. She stared at herself for a moment. Straight brown hair, tied up to keep it out of her face. Brown eyes. Plain features. Why couldn't she be classy like Becky, or beautiful like Jessica, or at least have stylish hair like Cathy? She stared at her reflection a little longer and then slowly went back to work.

By closing time, only two more customers had bothered to make their way inside the little bookstore. Mr. Lennard switched the sign so that it said "CLOSED" and locked the front door. Then he and Linda climbed into the green pickup truck and headed for home.

The Lennards' bookstore sat right at the edge of town. Three streets away and you were in farm country. Mr. Lennard took a couple side roads and soon arrived at their farm. The truck splashed into the muddy driveway and pulled up alongside the big, run-down, yellow house. The house had desperately needed a fresh coat of paint this past summer, but no one had found the time to do it. Mr. Lennard parked the truck, and Linda carefully stepped out trying hard not to sink into any mud puddles.

"Couldn't we do something about all this mud?" Linda couldn't help asking. "Every time it rains, this driveway becomes an enormous mud swamp."

"Speaking of mud, the driveway isn't the only mucky mess," Mrs. Lennard said, coming around the side of the house and looking unusually flustered. "Linda, I could really use your help. Supper's almost ready, and I really don't have time..."

Linda frowned in bewilderment until she saw her identical twin brothers...or what was left to see of them...come around the side of the house. Caked with mud from the crown of their brown-haired heads to their bare feet, the six-year-old boys looked like walking pieces of the driveway Linda was standing on. Linda stared at them in disbelief, and they stared down at their feet in embarrassment. It was hard to tell if they looked ashamed because they had been so thoughtless and naughty, or because they were standing before their father's stern gaze.

"We'll talk about this later, boys," Mr. Lennard finally said, walking past them toward the house. "Try to have them cleaned up in time for dinner, Linda," he added, entering the house with his wife.

Linda groaned as she led her brothers to the back of the house, and despite all their squealing and protesting, cleaned them off as best she could with the garden hose.

"How could you possibly get that dirty!" she scolded them as she brought them into the house, dried off their feet, and led them upstairs. "You knew you wouldn't be able to come into the house with that much mud all over you."

"We were just having fun," Micah whimpered.

"Micah threw mud on me, and I threw mud back, and we got in a mud fight, and we kept slipping and falling," Jonah explained. "We just thought it was fun."

"Well, it's not fun to clean it up," Linda grumbled.

After much effort, the twins were finally cleaned up, dried off, and dressed in clean, dry clothes. Linda combed their wet hair and then led them downstairs toward the waiting dinner table.

"Linda, can you pour the juice?" Amy asked as soon as Linda entered the bustling kitchen. "I still have to call Stephen in."

Linda took the pitcher from her sister and sidestepped her mother who was turning from the stove to place some more food on the table.

"Linda, will you help me study after dinner tonight? I have a really, really big test tomorrow, and I just know I'm going to fail!" Linda poured some juice into one of the glasses and then turned to face her overacting, twelve-year-old sister.

"Esther," she sighed. "How many times do I have to tell you? You're never going to get a good grade if you've already told yourself you're going to fail."

"I know, but it's soooo hard!" Esther wailed. "There's simply no possible way..."

"Linda!" nine-year-old Jane interrupted. "I can't find my pink slippers, and my feet are cold! Can you help me look for them?"

"I wouldn't know any better than you where to look for them," Linda replied, shrugging her shoulders. "Besides, it's almost time for dinner."

"Linda! Micah's in my seat, and he won't get up!" Jonah said, pointing at his twin brother and frowning indignantly.

"Why does it matter where you sit?" Linda asked, exasperated.

"Because that spot has the red cup, and I wanted the red cup!" Jonah whined.

"Well, why didn't you just say you wanted a red cup?" Linda asked, taking the blue cup off the table and replacing it with another red one. Satisfied, Jonah climbed into the chair next to his brother as Amy and Stephen entered the kitchen.

"Hey, Linda, don't worry about your farm chores tonight," Stephen said, taking off his jacket and hanging it on a hook. "I did 'em for you."

"Why?" Linda questioned, looking surprised.

Stephen shrugged. "It was only a couple things, and you did my chores last week when I was sick."

"Thanks, Steve," Linda said, joining the family around the dinner table. "You didn't have to."

The room grew quiet as the blessing was asked on the food, and then burst into noisy conversation once again as everyone began to eat.

Linda took a bite of her baked potato and stared out the window, secretly wishing she were somewhere else. It wasn't that she didn't like her family or didn't appreciate their company. It was just that amid conversations of bright red fire trucks, missing pink slippers, good grades, a newly repaired tractor engine, or even an upcoming graduation, she found herself feeling left out. After all, she was twenty-three now. She was no longer a child, and none of those things applied to her. Sometimes she felt as if she were living in a boarding house, sharing farm chores in exchange for a room.

After dinner, Linda helped clear the table. Fortunately, it was Amy and Esther's turn to wash dishes that night. Nevertheless, Linda spent the time she might have been doing dishes, helping Jane search for her precious slippers. When at last they were found, Linda immediately received a big, huge, suffocating hug from her little sister.

"Thanks, Linda!" Jane cried, joyfully. "You're the best!"

Linda wished there were some way she could be viewed as "the best" by more than just a nine-year-old. It was so easy to please her siblings. After all, she was their big sister. All she had to do was be there for them and they were happy. Why was it so much more difficult to gain respect among her peers? Why did they make her feel like such a loser? If finding her little sister's slippers was "the best" she could do…maybe they were right.

Linda spent the rest of the evening studying with Esther, and then put Jonah and Micah through their lengthy bedtime routine. Once they had finally settled in to sleep, Linda crept downstairs and announced she was going out to see the animals before she went to bed.

Stephen frowned as he watched his sister slip into her coat and race out into the night. Linda had been doing this for the past few nights, and he was beginning to get suspicious. What did she do out there when her chores were finished, and she had already seen the animals? Grabbing his coat, Stephen quietly left the house behind her.

Creeping across the grass, he could see a light was on in the cow barn. As he grew closer, he could hear Linda's voice. Who on earth was she talking to? Did she have a secret friend, or was she having a conversation with herself? Silently, Stephen reached the door and peeked inside.

"If only I could move on in life," Linda was saying. She was sitting on a stool in front of the cows. Was she talking to them?

"I'm tired of being nothing but a farm girl. How will I ever accomplish anything? All I know is, if opportunity ever comes knocking, I'm out of here!"

"You don't really mean that," Stephen said, sliding the barn door open and coming in. Linda jumped and stood up.

"Stephen!" she cried. "What…what are you doing?"

"What are *you* doing?" Stephen returned. "And what are you talking about?"

Linda sat back down as Stephen pulled up another stool and joined her.

"You wouldn't understand," Linda said, looking slightly embarrassed.

"Come on. I wanna know," Stephen prompted. "Are you planning to run away or something?"

Linda looked at her brother and sighed. "You have to promise me you won't say a word of this to anyone."

"I won't," Stephen promised. "When have I ever spilled a secret?"

Linda smiled. Her brother was right. He may be a snoop, but he could definitely keep a secret.

"I'm not going to run away," Linda assured him. "It's just that I have dreams I'd like to pursue that I'm afraid to even tell Mom or Dad about."

"Like what?" Stephen asked.

"Well, I've always wanted to act. I would love to pretend I'm someone I'm not. I mean, all my life amounts to is work, chores, and taking care of younger siblings. My life consists of nothing. I have no job, no income, no social life, and I'm not good at anything but finding slippers. I'm a loser, Steve. At least if I could pretend to be someone else, my life would seem more interesting."

"So, if you had an opportunity to become an actress, you would take it?" Stephen questioned.

"Within reason, but yes," Linda replied. "I would love to be in a play or something. I would love to be anyone but me."

"Your life does sound pretty unfair," Stephen agreed, "but hey, it'll get better sooner or later. I mean, someday you will get married, and then your life is bound to get better."

"Stephen, do you actually think anyone would see any potential in me?" Linda asked. "I have nothing to offer a guy. No one is ever going to want to marry me."

"God could make it happen," Stephen told her.

"Well, I know that," Linda said, shrugging. "But will He? What if He doesn't think I deserve anything better? I mean, I don't, really. I'm no better than anyone else. I just have to face the facts. Maybe it's not His will for me to be anything but a farm girl."

Chapter Three

Exciting News

Sunday morning, Linda walked into church, dreading what her three friends would say about Friday afternoon. She wished she could feel free to do what she wanted like they did, but instead, she felt imprisoned. Perhaps if she were good at something, her parents would allow her to pursue it, but she couldn't think of a single thing. Unfortunately, she was a "jack-of-all-trades, but master of none".

After delivering Jonah and Micah to their Sunday School class, Linda walked down the hall and entered the singles class. She still remembered when she and Michael had been in the youth group together. She had secretly dreaded the day when he would graduate to the singles class and leave her behind for two years. Of course, he had ended up leaving for college and moving away instead, which had turned out to be far worse.

Linda was about to take her seat when Mr. Donavan came walking up to her.

"Linda, would you mind playing the piano for us this morning?" he asked. "Jessica seems to be running late, and I can't wait much longer."

"Um, I only know 'Jesus Loves Me' and 'Amazing Grace'," Linda reminded him.

"Are you sure you haven't learned anything else?"

"I don't really have time to practice," Linda replied. "Those are the only songs I can play. I'm sorry."

"Well, I suppose 'Amazing Grace' will do," Mr. Donavan said, finally. "I don't know why Jessica hasn't been showing up on time."

As Linda made her way to the piano, she couldn't help but wonder if Jessica kept coming in late on purpose. Ever since she had been home from college, she had complained about the singles class' piano being junky and out of tune.

"All right! Let's get started this morning," Mr. Donavan announced. "I don't know where Jessica is, so I guess it's 'Amazing Grace' again. Let's sing it out!"

Linda sighed as she began the introduction. Once again, she was needed but not really wanted.

After making it through the song with only a couple mistakes, Linda returned to her seat.

"Okay, before we begin the lesson, I have a special announcement to make," Mr. Donavan said. "The other day, I received a phone call from someone I haven't heard from in a long time. How many of you remember my nephew, Michael Donavan?"

Linda's heart skipped a beat as she raised her hand. What was the announcement? Was he getting married? Linda swallowed hard as Mr. Donavan continued.

"He told me that he's been praying for the Lord's direction and guidance in his life and thought he would call and find out if there was anything he could help out with here. As you all know, we have been in prayer about a new Junior Church leader for a while now. Mr. and Mrs. Callahan have been doing it for a long time, and are eager to hand it over to someone younger. Well, I talked it over with Pastor Grant, and he has agreed to have Michael come out here and work under the Callahans for a while. If

Michael feels this is the Lord's will for him, he may end up taking it over."

By the time Mr. Donavan ended his announcement, Linda's heart was racing. Michael was coming back! After seven long years, she would finally get to see him again. What would he be like? Would he have changed? Would he still be someone she could admire? Then she paused. Was there any chance he would like her?

"Mr. Donavan, what will Michael be doing for a job?" Jessica asked, interrupting Linda's thoughts.

"When is he coming?" Becky asked.

"Where will he live?" Cathy joined in.

"And most importantly," Jessica added with a childish grin. "Is he still...single?"

"Girls, I can't answer all those questions yet," Mr. Donavan interrupted with a chuckle, "but, yes, he is still single."

Linda watched as Cathy, Becky, and Jessica all exchanged giddy grins. Apparently, Linda wasn't the only one who still held a fondness for Michael.

After Sunday School, Linda gathered her things and headed for the Junior Church classroom. She smiled inwardly as she thought about what it would be like to help out under Michael's leadership.

"Linda! Linda!"

Linda stopped and turned around.

"Can you believe Michael is coming back after all these years?" Cathy asked.

"It's been so long, I had almost forgotten about him," Becky said.

"How could you forget about Michael?" Jessica asked incredulously. "He was the sweetest guy in the whole church. Don't you agree, Linda?"

"Um, I…I…thought he was…really nice," Linda stammered.

"Really nice?" Cathy repeated. "Linda, everyone knows you've always secretly thought he was handsome."

"What?" Linda cried, blushing. "I…he…I always thought he was nicer than the other boys," she finally finished, nonchalantly. "He was…sensible."

"So you do like him!" Becky said, triumphantly.

"Well, maybe I do…kind of," Linda admitted. "What's wrong with that?"

"I don't know," Jessica replied. "We just thought maybe you weren't allowed to like guys." Then the three girls burst into giggles and continued down the hall. Linda frowned after them. What business of theirs was it to know whether she liked Michael or not? And of course she was allowed to like guys! She wasn't allowed to date them, but who ever said she couldn't like them?

When Linda entered the Junior Church classroom, Mrs. Callahan was right there to greet her.

"Hi, Linda," she said. "We're having a little bit of a problem today."

"What kind of problem?" Linda inquired, frowning. "It's not Jonah and Micah, is it?" she added quickly, searching the rows of chairs for her mischievous little brothers.

"Oh, no," Mrs. Callahan assured her. "It's that little girl over there in the purple shirt. She came in on the bus today, and she hasn't cooperated since the minute she set foot in our classroom. I don't know how we're going to get her settled down to start the class."

Linda turned to look in the direction Mrs. Callahan had pointed and almost immediately spotted the troublemaker. She looked about eight years old, and she had short, messy brown hair and a devious grin. At that very moment, she snatched another girl's Sunday School paper and tore it up.

"Okay, kids! It's time to sit down and be quiet! We're going to start now!" Mr. Callahan said, loudly from the front of the room.   Some of the noise and chaos dwindled as the children found their seats and waited to see what would happen first.

"I'll see what I can do," Linda whispered to Mrs. Callahan.

Making her way through the back row of girls, Linda sat down right next to the purple-shirted girl who was leaning forward, antagonizing the girl ahead of her.

"Hi," Linda whispered, tapping her on the shoulder. "I'm Miss Linda. What's your name?"

The little girl sat back hard in her chair. "I'm Kelly," she said a little louder than a whisper. "I don't want you to sit next to me."

"Why not?" Linda whispered as Mr. Callahan began leading the children in 'This Little Light of Mine'. There was no piano accompaniment, because Linda couldn't play that song, and Jessica refused to play "kiddy songs".

"I like to sit by myself!" Kelly replied, hopping up and marching to a different seat.

Linda remained seated, deciding it was probably better to keep an eye on her from a distance than disrupt the class with a game of musical chairs.

"All right, now we're going to hear a story from Miss Linda Lennard!" Mr. Callahan announced. "Linda?"

Linda quickly made her way to the front of the room. As she passed the third row, she glanced over just in time to see Kelly snatch a headband out of one of the girls' hair. Linda groaned inwardly as she began her short story. The entire time, Kelly fooled around, talked out loud, switched seats, and bothered everyone around her. How would she act once the lesson began?

Finishing her story, Linda returned to the fourth row and took a seat right behind Kelly. Soon, the lesson began, but Kelly continued to disrupt the other girls. Linda rolled her eyes, leaned forward, and tapped her on the shoulder.

"You need to be quiet while Mr. Callahan is talking," she whispered, gently.

"I don't have to listen to you!" Kelly hissed, folding her arms across her chest. She glared at Linda. "I thought I told you I didn't want to sit next to you!" she snapped.

"I'm not next to you. I'm behind you," Linda whispered, impatiently. "Now turn around and pay attention please."

"Go away!" Kelly demanded. "I don't want to pay attention! I'm bored!"

"Well, maybe if you were listening, you would find it a little more interesting," Linda suggested. "Shhh."

"I don't care about God! I don't care about church! And I don't care about you!" Kelly said, loudly.

"Take her out," Mrs. Callahan mouthed to Linda who glanced at her helplessly.

"Come with me," Linda whispered, standing up. She half expected Kelly to stubbornly refuse, but to her relief, she stood up and followed her out the side door and into the hall.

"Look," Linda said, crouching down to face Kelly. "You can't disrupt the class like this. Mr. Callahan's trying to talk to you kids, and you're just distracting everyone and not even listening."

"I don't want to listen! I don't even want to be here! I want to go home!" Kelly said, frowning indignantly.

"Well, if you don't care about God or church, and you don't want to be here, then why did you ride the bus?" Linda asked.

"Because my parents make me come!" Kelly burst out. "They want to get rid of me! They call Sunday mornings a vacation! They hate me!" Suddenly, she burst into tears. "Everybody hates me!" she wailed.

"Hey, hey. Please don't cry," Linda begged, giving her a hug. "I love you, and so does Jesus."

"Why would Jesus love me? I'm a bad girl, and…and I do bad things!"

"Jesus knows you do bad things," Linda told her. "That's why He died on the cross for you. He wants to forgive you for doing bad things, and if you're truly sorry, He will."

"Mr. Callahan said that bad people can't go to heaven," Kelly whimpered.

Linda grinned. "So you did listen a little," she said. "You should have kept listening. Mr. Callahan's right. Bad people can't go to heaven. But bad people who are sorry for what they've done and ask Jesus to save them from it, can go to heaven."

"I am sorry!" Kelly sniffed. "I want Jesus to save me! Do you really think He will?"

Linda looked right into the little girl's searching and earnest eyes and said, "I *know* He will."

Linda knelt down on the floor with her, and Kelly began to pray. "Jesus," she began. "I'm a bad girl, and nobody likes me. Miss Linda says you love me though, and she says you'll save me if I'm sorry. I am sorry! Please save me so I can go to heaven. Amen."

Kelly opened her eyes and Linda hugged her. "Are you ready to go back into class now?" she asked.

"Yeah! I want to tell Mr. Callahan that I got saved!" Kelly answered.

By the time they re-entered the classroom, Mr. Callahan had just finished the closing prayer and was about to dismiss the children.

"Mr. Callahan!" Kelly shouted. "I just got saved!"

Chapter Four

A Competition

Wednesday morning, Mr. Lennard went to work in the bookstore by himself. Wednesday was Linda's day to help out at home. Stephen was in the cow barn milking cows, and Linda was giving them more feed.

"Stephen, do you remember Michael Donavan?" she asked, dumping a pail of feed into one of the troughs.

"Who?" Stephen asked.

"Michael Donavan," Linda repeated. "He was two years older than me, and he left for college seven years ago. Then his family moved out of state, so we never saw him again."

"I would have only been eight when he left, but I kind of remember him. We had a picnic as a going-away party, right?"

"Yeah," Linda said. "Well, I just heard on Sunday that he's coming back. He's going to work with the Callahans in Junior Church."

"Is he married?"

"No."

"That's interesting."

"Interesting?" Linda repeated, turning to frown quizzically at her brother.

"Do you think maybe he will marry you?" Stephen asked, bluntly.

"I...I don't know," Linda replied, blushing. "He might consider it. I mean, what are the chances of him all of a sudden coming back after all these years? Maybe Dad's right. When you wait for God's choice, they do fall right into your lap."

"Do you like him?" Stephen asked, suddenly.

"I've always liked him," Linda admitted, honestly. "The question is, will he like me?"

"I think he will," Stephen said, shrugging. He leaned down to continue his milking. "Why wouldn't he?"

"I don't know," Linda replied. "I'm not very pretty." Her brown hair hung in a long braid down the middle of her back, and a few messy strands had escaped and hung loosely around her face. She looked down at her dirty, brown, farm skirt. "Let's just say I'd never win any beauty contests. That's for sure."

"Well, if it's a beauty queen he's looking for, he's pretty shallow," Stephen pointed out. "Look, Linda. If Michael Donavan is looking for God's choice, it's not going to matter how pretty you are. Besides, you're not ugly."

"Thanks, Stephen," Linda said. "How does my little brother always know just what to say?" she added with a grin.

"By quoting Dad!" Stephen replied, laughing.

"So, you just like to think you're smart!" Linda returned, running toward her brother.

Stephen jumped up from his stool and avoided Linda's whack. "You're scaring the cows!" he laughed as the nervous animals began mooing loudly and shifting in protest.

"Oh, come on. You know I wouldn't hurt you," Linda told them. "I was only playing."

Stephen finished the milking, and then went inside to start school. Linda spent the rest of the morning cleaning the house and helping the twins with their school work. After lunch, she took them upstairs to get them ready for their nap.

"We're too old to take naps!" Jonah protested. "I wanna play outside!"

"If you had spent most of the morning vacuuming, dusting, scrubbing sinks, and mopping floors, you would be tired enough to want a nap," Linda told them.

"Well, we didn't vacuum, or scrub, or anything, so we're not tired enough to want a nap," Micah said.

"We promise not to be whiney tonight!" Jonah whined. "Can't we skip our nap?"

"No," Linda said. "It's nap time, and you're not getting out of it no matter how much you beg. Now, lie still and close your eyes."

When the twins had finally settled in, Linda went downstairs. Stephen was outside, cleaning the chicken coop, and Esther and Jane were in the kitchen, washing dishes.

"Linda!" Mrs. Lennard called from the living room. "Why don't you come help me fold this laundry?"

Linda entered the room to find her mother sitting on the couch surrounded by three overflowing baskets of clothes waiting to be folded. Amy was across the room, ironing dress shirts, skirts, and dresses.

Linda sat down and pulled the twins' matching red and blue shirts out of one of the baskets. "Mom, do you remember Michael Donavan?" she asked.

"Michael Donavan? Sure I do. I remember the whole Donavan family quite well," her mother replied. "They were a nice family. I was sad to see them go, but when God calls you to a different ministry, it's best to obey."

Linda nodded. "Well, I just heard that Michael is returning," she said. "He's looking for the Lord's leading, and he's going to help the Callahans in Junior Church for a while. He may end up taking it over if He feels that's what God would have him do."

Mrs. Lennard smiled. "You've liked him since we first came to the church when you were in second grade." She sighed. "It's been a long time. Is he married?"

"No," Linda answered.

"Let me guess. You're hoping he'll marry you, right?" Amy said from across the room.

"Well, it…it would be nice to finally be married and have a family of my own," Linda admitted. "I just don't know if I'm the kind of girl he would want. I don't even know if anyone would want a girl like me. I mean, Cathy, Becky, and Jessica have so much more to offer someone. I'm not good at anything."

"You're good at housework," Mrs. Lennard pointed out. "I don't think any of those girls would dare put their pretty little nails to a scrub brush."

"I know, but I'm talking about something impressive," Linda told her. "If I could play an instrument well, or if I was good at drawing, or painting, or sewing, maybe someone would find me more interesting."

"Linda, when the right man comes along, they're going to like you for who you are; not what you can do," Mrs. Lennard assured her. "He will be so busy trying to impress you, he won't even care about what you have to impress him with."

Linda gave her an unsure smile. "I hope you're right, Mom," she said. "Do you think Michael will remember me?"

"Of course he will!" Mrs. Lennard said. "He wasn't blind! Linda, you stand out more than you realize. Don't always think so little of yourself. You need to stop comparing yourself to what those friends of yours think you should be, and concentrate on what God wants you to be."

Linda sighed. She knew her mother was right, but it was so hard to believe that being a loser was all God wanted her to be.

Later that evening, Linda and her family arrived at church for the Wednesday night service. In the lobby, Linda's three friends stood in a group, chattering excitedly.

"Linda!" Cathy called, waving her over. Linda broke from her family and walked over to join them.

"Guess what we just heard?" Becky announced. "Michael will be here a week from today!"

"We were just discussing which of us will be the lucky choice for Michael's bride!" Jessica said.

"Michael's bride?" Linda repeated. "How do you know he's coming here to look for a wife?"

"Why else would God lead him right back to our little country church where there are so many available young ladies?" Jessica asked.

"The question is, will he want a waitress, a seamstress, or a professional pianist?" Cathy mused.

"What about me?" Linda asked. "I'm available too."

"Linda, not to hurt your feelings or anything, but...you don't exactly have anything going for you," Becky stated, hesitantly. "Michael will be looking for someone useful. Someone who can add to his life."

"But...but...I'm good at housework," Linda faltered.

"If Michael only wanted someone to take care of his house, he could just hire a servant," Jessica said. "Face it, Linda. You're just not cut out to be married. I suggest you drop out of the competition while you're still ahead."

"It's not a competition!" Linda cried. "Marriage is a serious commitment! Not a contest!"

"You do need credibility though," Becky insisted. "Not to be blunt, but you don't really have any."

"I thought you guys were my friends," Linda choked out, fighting back tears.

"We are your friends," Cathy said. "That's why we're warning you ahead of time."

"I have just as much hope of marrying Michael as you do!" Linda told them. "In fact, I have even more hope, because I'm not playing games!"

"Just stay out of our way, Linda," Becky warned.

Jessica gave a rude little chuckle. "Look, girls. All Linda has going for her is her ability to serve, and that's not exactly something that stands out. She may think she's in this competition, but Michael won't even give her a second glance."

Chapter Five

The Missionary

Saturday morning, Linda was in the bookstore, helping her dad restock the shelves with new books. She had been in a sulky mood ever since Wednesday night when her friends had decided to betray her. She should have known it was coming. They had never thought much of her even when they were growing up. She had always been the loser of the group.

"Linda." Linda jumped. She had been so lost in her own thoughts; she had forgotten that her father was right beside her. "You've been pretty quiet all morning," he said. "Is something on your mind?"

Linda sighed. How could she possibly explain to her dad how she felt? After all, it was mostly his doing. If it weren't for his strict rules, and constant supervision, she may have made something of herself by now.

"Your mother told me about Michael Donavan," Mr. Lennard said. "If I remember right, he was a fine young man."

Linda nodded in agreement and placed another book on the shelf.

"She also mentioned that you are quite fond of him," Mr. Lennard added.

Linda nodded again.

"Have you considered the idea that he could possibly be the right one for you?" Mr. Lennard asked.

"It doesn't matter," Linda replied, sadly. "Cathy, Becky, and Jessica have decided that it's a competition to win Michael's heart. They're going to do everything they can to impress him, and they told me to stay out of their way, because I don't have a chance."

Mr. Lennard frowned. "I thought they were your friends?"

"So did I," Linda agreed. "They're right though," she said, as tears began to sting her eyes. "I don't stand a chance against them. When you have a choice between a successful waitress, a professional seamstress, and a beautiful pianist, who would choose a plain farm girl loser like me? That's who I am, Dad. Linda the loser. Nobody's ever going to see any potential in me."

"Linda, how many times must we go through this?" Mr. Lennard questioned. "I don't ask others to agree with me, but I strongly believe a girl's place is in her home until the day she marries. There is far too much danger in the world for a girl to be out there all on her own."

"Cathy, Becky, and Jessica haven't run into any trouble," Linda pointed out.

"That doesn't mean it couldn't happen to you," Mr. Lennard warned. "Besides, your family needs you, Linda. Would it be fair for you to leave your place and your duties to go pursue some selfish dream of your own?"

"Dad, how can you say it's selfish to pursue something?" Linda asked as tears began to moisten her eyelashes.

"It's selfish to leave people behind who need you," Mr. Lennard insisted, gently. "Linda, I wish I could make you understand. If God wanted you to pursue something, He would open the door."

Just then, the little bell on the front door jingled downstairs.

"Linda, I didn't mean to make you upset," Mr. Lennard said, placing a hand gently on his crying daughter's trembling shoulder. "I just…I…try to calm down. We have a customer." Then he left her side and made his way downstairs. Linda could hear him greeting the customer.

"Hello, Sir. I'm Andrew Lennard. How do you do?"

Linda took in a deep breath and wiped the tears from her eyes and face. Why couldn't her father see how sad he made her? Couldn't he at least compromise a little? Did he really only force her to stay at home because they needed her? Was she really nothing but a slave to them?

It took Linda half an hour to finish shelving the rest of the books. She stood up to stretch, and then looked at the clock. It was noon, and her dad had still not come upstairs. Was the customer still there? And why hadn't they come upstairs to look around?

"Linda! Come downstairs! I'd like you to meet someone!"

Linda obediently walked down the stairs, thankful that she had been given enough time to recover from her crying.

"Linda, this is Mr. White. Mr. White, my oldest daughter, Linda," Mr. Lennard introduced.

"It's nice to meet you," Mr. White said with a friendly smile. He stepped forward and shook Linda's hand. He was a tall man with gray hair and kind eyes.

"Mr. White is a missionary to the Philippines," Mr. Lennard explained. "He will be speaking at our church tomorrow."

"If you don't mind my asking, how old are you, Linda?" Mr. White inquired.

"Twenty-three," Linda answered.

Mr. White smiled but said nothing. "I wonder," he said, suddenly addressing Mr. Lennard. "Would you and your daughter like to join me for lunch at the restaurant down the street? I'd like to hear more about your family and your church."

"Of course," Mr. Lennard replied. "Linda and I would enjoy that very much."

About fifteen minutes later, Linda, her father, and Mr. White had arrived at the restaurant and placed their orders. As they waited for the food to come, Mr. White continued to ask about the Lennard family.

"How many children do you have?"

"There are seven including Linda," Mr. Lennard replied. "Linda is twenty-three, Amy is eighteen, Stephen is fifteen, Esther is twelve, Jane is nine, and…how old are Jonah and Micah now?" He turned to Linda with a frown.

"They're six," Linda told him.

"Both of them?" Mr. White asked, raising one eyebrow at Linda.

"Yes, they're identical twins," Linda explained, although she could tell by the twinkle in his eye that Mr. White had already guessed.

"So, you're the oldest of seven. That must come with a lot of responsibility."

Linda looked up into this kind man's eyes. How did he know? "Yes, it does," she answered slowly.

"I was the oldest of five," Mr. White explained. "I know what it's like to be responsible for more than just yourself. It seems unfair at times, but it tends to build character. I know it did for me."

Linda was surprised. This man understood things about her that she feared even her parents didn't understand.

While they ate their food, Mr. Lennard told Mr. White a little bit about the church. "It's a fairly small, country church," he said. "Only about seventy-five members. We've attended there almost sixteen years."

"My, that's quite a long time," Mr. White commented, looking surprised. Then he turned to Linda. "Do you have a job of any kind?"

Linda lowered her eyes. "No," she answered. "Well, I work with my father in the bookstore of course."

Mr. White nodded. "It's a fine bookstore," he said. "You should consider it an honor to be a part of it."

"Linda also helps us an awful lot at home," Mr. Lennard put in. "We own a farm, so there are always many chores to be done. It will be hard to lose her."

"I can imagine," Mr. White said. "You know, I've only met one other girl like you before, Linda. They're hard to find these days. Young ladies who are willing to serve under their parents' leadership are almost completely unheard of. I am impressed when I happen to run across one."

Linda lowered her head. She knew she hadn't exactly been willing to, and she felt a little guilty accepting praise.

Mr. White and Mr. Lennard continued to converse throughout the remainder of the meal, and then Mr. White insisted on paying the bill.

"But you're the missionary," Mr. Lennard objected. "I can't allow you to do that."

"I am a single man though," Mr. White pointed out. "You have a wife and seven children. Besides, I've very much enjoyed meeting you and your daughter."

Mr. Lennard and Linda waited while Mr. White paid, and then they walked together to their vehicles.

"Well, I'll see you at church tomorrow," Mr. White said, opening the front door of his car. "Oh, Linda. Are you by any chance...seeing anyone yet?"

"No," Linda replied, realizing he was referring to a young man. "I haven't found the right one yet."

"Well, I'm sure that right person is out there somewhere," Mr. White assured her. "When God sees that you're both ready, He will bring you together. That's how He works. Divine betrothal they call it. God takes two people and betroths them in His own Divine way."

"Divine betrothal. I like that," Mr. Lennard said. "I've never heard that before."

"It's getting around," Mr. White told him. "The key is, your heart has to be right. That's when God starts to work." He winked at Linda. "You're going to make someone a very fine wife," he added. Then he climbed into his car, said goodbye, and drove away.

Chapter Six

My Father's Servant

The next day, Linda arrived at church feeling a little disappointed. She enjoyed helping out in Junior Church, but she was really looking forward to hearing Mr. White preach. Unfortunately, she would just have to wait until the evening service. At least Jessica had made it to Sunday School early for once and would be available to play the piano in their class.

"Linda," Jessica said, walking up to Linda. As usual, Cathy and Becky came right along with her. "We wanted to apologize for the other day," Jessica continued, slowly. "We realized we were a little harsh. I mean, we never wanted to hurt your feelings or anything."

"We just didn't want you to get your hopes up and then have them dashed to pieces," Cathy finished, sounding a little too sympathetic.

"It's okay," Linda said, shrugging. "You guys were right. There's nothing to like about me."

"Well, we wanted to make it up to you," Becky offered, "by giving you a little suggestion."

"A…a suggestion?" Linda repeated. She didn't exactly feel right about this, but she was curious nonetheless. What were they up to?

"You see, Linda," Cathy said, sitting down next to her. "You need something that will be useful or helpful to a guy. Something that will make you worth his interest."

"That's not your only problem though," Becky put in. "You also need to convince your dad that you need something."

"That's impossible," Linda objected, shaking her head sadly. "He refuses to budge."

"Then you will have to be very persuasive," Becky prompted.

"What exactly did you have in mind?" Linda inquired, looking questioningly from one girl to the other.

"Well," Jessica began, "it's like this. Your dad won't let you pursue anything, because he thinks it would be selfish, right?"

"Kind of," Linda replied.

"So, why not go to college to become a teacher?" Jessica continued. "That way, you would acquire some sort of usefulness, but at the same time, you would also be helping others. Your dad couldn't possibly see that as selfish, could he?"

"I don't know," Linda said, sounding unsure. "My dad doesn't believe in girls getting jobs out in the world."

Becky rolled her eyes. "How can he be so protective!" she exclaimed.

"Look," Cathy cut in. "This is where it gets good. See, you wouldn't be getting your teaching degree, so you could get a job out in the world. You would be getting your teaching degree, so you could better home school any future children you may have."

"It's a foolproof plan," Becky said. "A girl with a teaching degree would be very impressive to a guy, and your dad can't possibly see anything wrong with it."

Linda thought for a moment. It did sound foolproof. Was there really a chance her dad might go along with it?

"I guess it's worth a try," she finally admitted.

"Of course it is," Jessica agreed, confidently. "I would suggest you talk to your dad about it as soon as possible."

"If I go to college now, I won't be here very long after Michael comes," Linda pondered aloud.

"Well, that's okay," Cathy said, quickly. "You already agreed that there's nothing he would find impressive about you. He wouldn't care about you until you've gone to college anyway."

"That's true," Linda agreed reluctantly. She wasn't real sure about this plan, but then, what did she have to lose?

Just then, class started, and Jessica made her way to the "out of tune" piano. After Sunday School, Linda went directly to Junior Church. Kelly greeted her with a big hug and asked her to sit beside her. Linda couldn't believe how much better she behaved compared to last week. She still wiggled around and whispered occasionally, but her sour attitude was completely gone.

On the way home that afternoon, Linda contemplated when would be the best time to suggest the college plan to her dad. Should she announce it with all of her family members present, or should she talk to him alone? She thought about it the whole time she helped her mother and sisters prepare the afternoon meal, and by the time they sat down to eat, she had made her decision.

"Dad, I've decided I'd like to go to college," she spilled out in the most confident voice she could muster.

"Linda, we've already talked about this," Mr. Lennard said. "I do not see any good in sending a girl off to college. As far as I'm concerned, young ladies have no business gallivanting off into the world, pursuing their own selfish desires."

"No, Dad, you don't understand!" Linda said, quickly. "I'd like to go to college to become a teacher. That way, I could be better at home schooling any future children I might have."

"Where did you get an idea like that?" Mr. Lennard asked. "You help home school your brothers and sisters, and you do just fine. You don't need to waste four years of your life learning something you already know. I think you're trying to impress someone. Am I right?"

"Ooooo, who is he?" Amy asked.

"Do we know him?" Esther piped in.

"Dad, you can't keep me here as your slave forever!" Linda cried. "It's not fair! I have a life! Don't I have a right to live it? I'm tired of being a loser! Please let me do something with my life!"

"Linda, I will not have you talking to me like that in front of the other children! Please leave the table, and we'll discuss this later," Mr. Lennard ordered.

Linda fled from the room and burst into tears. She spent the rest of the afternoon in her bedroom, crying. She kept expecting her father to come up and talk with her, but he never came.

He's probably really upset, she thought, sitting up to look at the time. They would have to leave in half an hour to make it to the evening church service.

Linda sighed and began to freshen up for church. She felt completely crushed. Not only did she have to give up any hope of ever becoming anything of value to anyone, but also her father was angry with her. She should have known he was far too smart to be fooled into a plan like that, even if it was foolproof. Now, there was only one person left whom she could turn to for hope of ever escaping her lonely and miserable life.

God, she prayed silently as she left her bedroom. *Help me understand why you've chosen this life for me.*

As the Lennard family filed out their front door for church, Mr. Lennard laid a hand on Linda's shoulder.

"I spoke too rashly," he said, softly. "Let's talk tomorrow when we've both had some time to think things over."

"Okay," Linda replied, with a weak smile.

When they got to church, Linda purposely avoided any contact with Cathy, Becky, or Jessica. She wasn't ready to tell them that their "foolproof" plan had backfired. As she sat down for the service, she mentally resigned herself to the fact that she would never amount to anything successful. It wasn't even worth worrying about anymore. Her lot in life had already been chosen, and there was obviously nothing she could do to change it. She fought to control a small wave of bitterness sweeping over her as everyone stood for the opening hymn.

Why me? she thought. *Why did God choose a life like this for me?*

Quickly, Linda pushed her feelings aside in order to concentrate on the service. She smiled a little when Mr. White finally stepped behind the pulpit to begin his sermon. He had entitled it "My Father's

Servant". Linda listened intently as he began to tell stories of single women in the Bible, and their service to both their earthly fathers and Heavenly Father. He began with Genesis chapter twenty-four and recounted the story of Rebekah's marriage to Isaac. He pointed out that Rebekah had been fetching water for her father's household when she was chosen to be Isaac's wife. He told the story in Genesis chapter twenty-nine involving Jacob's love for Rachel. He noted in verse nine that Rachel was caring for her father's sheep when Jacob first met her. He told the story in the book of Esther, explaining how Esther's parents had died, but she submitted herself to her cousin, Mordecai, as if he were her father.

"Lastly, I would like to mention Ruth the Moabitess," Mr. White concluded. "The Bible never really says whether Ruth's father was still alive, but it was her mother-in-law whom she submitted herself to. In doing so, Ruth not only gave up her native country, but she also made a decision to serve the one, true God over any false gods her native people served. Ruth became a wonderful example of a servant and was later rewarded with a husband and child.

"You see, God rewards those who truly demonstrate a submissive heart. These ladies I've mentioned tonight were servants to their earthly fathers and/or Heavenly Father, and God rewarded them. If there's anything God finds impressive, it's a servant. In Matthew twenty-three and verse eleven, Jesus said, 'But he that is greatest among you shall be your servant.'

"I want to finish with this closing statement. If you ever come to a place where you're just not sure what God wants you to do with your life, just be your Father's servant."

Chapter Seven

Repentance

Linda had felt the growing conviction of the Holy Spirit throughout Mr. White's entire sermon, and now, as everyone stood for prayer, she felt a desperate need to find a place at the altar and confess her unsubmissive spirit. She hadn't been a servant to her earthly father or her Heavenly Father, and she certainly hadn't exhibited a submissive spirit. Lately, all she had thought about was herself.

As soon as the invitation began, Linda walked down the aisle and knelt in front of the altar.

Lord, she prayed. *Please forgive me for not submitting to my father. I don't understand his ways or his thinking, but that's no excuse for not accepting his decisions for my life. Please help me to be a better servant, not only to my father and his wishes, but also to you, Lord. I realized tonight that I don't have to be able to do any one thing well in order to serve you. All I have to do is submit to my father and be helpful to others. Please make me a better servant for you. In your name, Amen.*

As Linda stood up and made her way back to her seat, she felt as if she had an entirely new outlook on life. Why hadn't she noticed before that all those ladies in the Bible had been servants? She still didn't exactly understand her father's motives for being so strict with her, but at least now she knew the right thing to do. She would apologize to her father and no longer grumble about his decisions. He had said they would talk tomorrow. Yes. That's when she would tell him.

Monday morning, Linda stood shivering beside her father while he unlocked the front door of the bookstore. The weather seemed to be getting colder as November approached, but at least there was no precipitation.

Mr. Lennard turned the knob and pushed the door open. Flicking on the lights, he shed his coat as Linda followed him inside and closed the door. Once inside, Linda removed her coat and hung it up beside her father's.

"Let's go upstairs and finish unpacking those last couple boxes of books in the storeroom," Mr. Lennard said, heading for the staircase.

"Dad, I need to talk to you," Linda said as they reached the second floor.

"I know," Mr. Lennard said, nodding his head in agreement. "Too late, I realized that I never even gave you a chance. Tell me again why you want to go to college?"

"No, it's…it's not that," Linda told him. "I…I need to apologize. I was convicted last night during Mr. White's sermon. Dad, I haven't been the servant I should be to you or to God." Her eyes welled up with tears as she continued. "I'm so sorry for not being submissive to you and your decisions for my life. I promise to honor your wishes from now on. I was wrong to wish for anything different. I hope you'll forgive me."

"Linda, of course I forgive you," Mr. Lennard said, giving her a hug. "I'm also happy to hear that you've gotten things settled. I…I think it's time I told you a very important story."

Mr. Lennard led Linda over to the window seat, and they both sat down.

"Is this a true story?" Linda asked.

"I wish it weren't," Mr. Lennard sighed. "It's also a very sad story. Did you know I had a sister named Linda?"

"No," Linda answered, looking surprised. She knew of her Uncle Rob and Aunt Martha, but she had never heard of an Aunt Linda.

"Linda was always my favorite sister growing up," Mr. Lennard continued. "I suppose it had something to do with her being the oldest and I the youngest. Anyway, she spent a lot of time with me, caring for me and such. She was ten years older than me, so she was thirteen by the time I was three. I have a lot of fond memories of her."

"What happened?" Linda asked, searchingly.

"Well, she grew up," Mr. Lennard answered. "She got to be eighteen and, as far as I knew, she still cared for me. Of course, I was eight by then. I didn't need as much care, but she still spent time with me. Then one day, I overheard her talking to our father. She was upset, and she was demanding that she be allowed to move out of the house and get a job. My father didn't approve, but she moved out anyway. I begged her not to. I was heartbroken. She promised me I could come and visit whenever I wanted. Somehow I knew things wouldn't ever be the same.

"After Linda got a job working at a restaurant in the mall, she became very close friends with one of her male co-workers. They even started to consider marriage. Well, it turns out this friend of hers was involved with a group of criminals. He and his friends broke into Linda's apartment one night while she was at our house, visiting us. It almost felt like old times that night. Our father had finally given up on trying to force her to move back home, and she spent some quality time with us." Mr. Lennard paused almost as if the memories were more than he could bear.

"Linda left late that night to return to her apartment," he went on. "When she got there, the three masked burglars were just finishing their job. She walked in on them, and one of them was so frightened, he pulled a gun out and killed her."

Linda gasped. Her eyes widened in shock, and she stared at her father in disbelief. Certainly that couldn't have possibly been a true story! She stared into her father's saddened eyes and realized for the first time why he had always been so over-protective of her. Those were the same sad eyes that Linda had stared into that day when she had begged to go to the mall with her friends. The same sad eyes that she stared into every time she begged for more freedom. Why hadn't she seen it before? Why hadn't it meant anything to her? But then, how could she have possibly known?

"Why didn't you tell me that story before?" Linda asked. "Maybe I...maybe I could have understood better."

"Linda," Mr. Lennard replied. "For one thing, it's a very difficult story for me to tell. I lost one of my closest friends that day. Also, I wanted you to learn to be submissive without having to know all the reasons. When I realized you had done that, I decided to tell you."

"I'm glad you did," Linda said, quietly. "I had decided to be submissive anyway, but I still didn't understand why you were so strict about where I went and what I did."

"I love you, Linda, and I wouldn't ever want anything to happen to you. There are times when you will never know the extent of someone's love. If I had chosen never to tell you the story of your Aunt Linda, you never would have known how much love was behind my seemingly overbearing decisions."

Linda nodded. "I'm sorry, Dad. I should have been more understanding anyway. I guess I was just so blinded by the aspect of Michael coming back. Cathy, Becky, and Jessica's competition had me distracted too. I was sure I was going to lose if I didn't find a more productive life."

"Linda, I believe what Mr. White said about Divine betrothal. I want God to betroth you to the person He has chosen. If that person is Michael, it won't matter what kind of competition those girls think they're in. Trust God, Linda. He never fails."

"Thanks, Dad," Linda said, smiling up at him.

Just then, the bell above the front door gave a clang. Linda and her father jumped and then grinned.

"Let's get back to work," Mr. Lennard suggested, patting Linda's shoulder.

Chapter Eight

Michael's Return

Wednesday night, Linda walked into church with a flutter in her stomach. This was the first night she would get to see Michael after seven years. It was true she had finally decided to submit to the life her dad had chosen for her, but she couldn't help facing the fact that compared to Cathy, Becky, and Jessica, she still felt like a loser. They had come such a long way since the last time Michael had seen them, and yet she was still the same old farm girl she had been when he'd left. Maybe she should just avoid him. After all, that's what Cathy, Becky, and Jessica wanted. Besides, it would save her the embarrassment of admitting she was nothing more than the child he had known seven years ago.

As the Lennard family made their way into the semi-crowded church lobby, Linda glanced around anxiously, wondering if Michael had arrived yet. Suddenly, she felt a light tap on her arm and almost jumped. It was Stephen.

"Is that Michael?" he whispered.

Linda looked in the direction her brother was pointing and saw Cathy, Becky, and Jessica surrounding a young man wearing a blue suit and grinning. Linda's heart leaped. It *was* Michael!

Linda quietly walked over until she was a few feet away from the chattering little huddle. She was hoping to get close enough to overhear what they were saying while still going unnoticed. Just as she was counting on, no one even glanced her way.

"I'm very much looking forward to hearing you play the piano," Michael was telling Jessica. "Last time I heard you, you were very good. I can hardly imagine what you must sound like now."

"Well, there's hardly a piece of music I can't play," Jessica replied with a fake-sounding chuckle. She was obviously enjoying Michael's flattery.

"You should stop by my seamstress shop, Michael," Becky said to him. "Maybe I could tailor you a suit coat. I could really use the practice, and it would be fun."

"If you ever decide to eat at the restaurant I work at, my hours are usually four-thirty to eight," Cathy put in. "If you'd like to come while I'm working there," she added, quickly.

"You girls have been really busy, that's for sure!" Michael said with a laugh. "I can hardly believe how much you've accomplished in such a short time."

"Don't forget. You've been gone seven years," Jessica reminded him. "To some of us, that can seem like an awfully long time."

"We've really missed you, Michael," Cathy added.

"You aren't planning on leaving again any time soon, are you?" Becky asked.

"At least, if you did decide to leave again," Jessica ventured, slowly, "perhaps you…wouldn't have to go away alone."

Linda had to catch herself before letting out a gasp. She was shocked that Jessica would dare to be so bold.

Michael grinned awkwardly. "I…I'll keep that in mind," he responded.

Linda turned away. She couldn't bear to hear any more. Michael may have been a little taken aback by Jessica's forceful approach, but there was no doubt he was very impressed by the girls' accomplishments. Linda wished she had something new and exciting to talk about, but instead, she was still her same old self.

Sadly, she wandered into the auditorium and sat down beside her family. As soon as the service was over, Linda inwardly hoped her father wouldn't be in the mood to stick around. She turned around and searched the large room just in time to see Michael leave through the back door followed by the three ambitious competitors. Linda looked on in disgust.

"So," Stephen whispered, coming up beside her. "Did you talk to him?"

"Don't be ridiculous," Linda mumbled back. "What on earth would I tell him? Cathy, Becky, and Jessica have already filled him in on all the wonderful things they've been doing. What could I possibly say that he would want to hear?"

Stephen shrugged. "Maybe he would like a turn to talk about what he's been doing," he suggested.

"Linda," Micah said, tugging on Linda's sleeve. "Me and Jonah want you to take us to the drinking fountain. We're thirsty."

"Ask Amy to take you," Linda told her brothers.

"But she's already gone," Jonah objected. "Please, Linda?"

"Oh, all right," Linda said, giving in. "Come on."

She took her brothers by the hands and led them out of the auditorium and down the hall to the drinking fountain.

"I get to drink first!" Jonah announced, stepping up ahead of Micah.

Micah started to object, but Linda stopped him. "Take turns," she warned.

"Yeah, and leave some for me," Michael added with a chuckle.

Linda turned just in time to see him walk up beside them. Her eyes fell to the floor uncertainly, but then she looked up again.

"Hi, Michael," she said.

"Hi, Linda," Michael replied. "I guess I missed you earlier. I mean, I saw you, but I didn't get a chance to talk to you. Don't tell me you're already married with kids!" He laughed and nodded toward the twins.

"Don't be silly!" Linda laughed. "Of course I'm not married. Those are my brothers."

Michael grinned. "Just making sure. So, what's new with you?"

"Oh, not much," Linda answered, her face growing serious once again. She had been hoping to avoid that question.

"Your dad still own the farm and that bookstore of his?" Michael asked.

"Yes," Linda responded.

"I'm sure you help with that a whole lot," Michael noted.

"Yes, I do."

"Have you attended college at all?"

Linda sighed. "No. My father doesn't agree with girls making a career for themselves."

Michael frowned slightly, but didn't respond. "So, nothing's really changed since the last time we saw each other."

Linda shook her head. "The only thing that's new with me is a couple of calves born on the farm last spring!"

"What about a couple new brothers?" Michael asked, pointing at Jonah and Micah. "I don't remember your mother having twins."

"Jonah and Micah were born about a year after you left," Linda explained.

"Is that so?" Michael said, looking down at them. "Well, if you two don't mind, I'd like to take a turn at the drinking fountain."

Linda gently led her brothers away from the drinking fountain. As Michael grinned and stooped down to drink, Linda noticed

Cathy, Becky, and Jessica heading down the hall toward them.

"I should really be going," Linda said quickly. She took the twins' hands and began to back away from Michael. "My father will probably want to leave soon, since we have to get up early and tend to the farm chores."

"Yeah, see you around," Michael told her, watching the three Lennards hurry back down the hall in the opposite direction of Michael's three admirers. The last thing Linda wanted was to talk to Michael with Cathy, Becky, and Jessica right there to brag about their accomplishments in comparison to her failures. Could Michael ever see any potential in her?

Chapter Nine

"Behold, The Handmaid Of The Lord."

"All right, everyone! Listen up! I have a very special announcement to make," Mr. Donavan announced one Sunday morning. "This Christmas will be our first year ever to put on a church Christmas play!"

"Oh!" Jessica squealed. "That will be so fun!"

"Our singles class will be performing the play which has been written by my nephew, Michael," Mr. Donavan explained.

"Michael, I didn't know you could write plays!" Becky exclaimed. "When did you write it?"

"I had to write one in college," Michael replied. "It was a lot of fun. I just hope everyone will be able to learn their parts in time. It's the beginning of November already."

"Well," Mr. Donavan continued, "tonight, Michael would like everyone who is interested in participating to meet him here in our classroom after the evening service. He will explain more then."

"What's the main girl character's name?" Jessica asked, excitedly.

"Mary," Mr. Donavan replied.

"Oh, it's the Christmas story! Jesus' birth," Cathy concluded.

"That's right," Michael told her. "All the lines will be exact quotes from the Bible except for parts that weren't recorded in detail."

"Like when they come to the inn and find out there's no room for them," Becky said.

"Exactly," Michael responded.

"I just know I'm going to get the part of Joseph," said Ken Richardson, who had just recently turned twenty-seven. "I hardly need to try out for it."

"I wouldn't be so sure about that," Jared Blake objected. "I'll be trying for that part too." He was a year younger than Ken, and the two had been friends for years.

"Just wait," Michael said, grinning. "Tryouts will be held on Tuesday."

Linda could hardly believe her ears. She would have the chance to participate in a real play! It was almost like a dream come true! Even a small part would be exciting, but she secretly hoped she might be chosen to play the part of Mary.

After Sunday School, Linda made her way to the Junior Church classroom. Michael was already there, and to Linda's dismay, Jessica. She was chattering away excitedly about the play while Michael listened eagerly. Of course, he would be thrilled to know that someone was so interested in his play. If only he knew how much it meant to her.

She sat down as Michael took his position at the front of the classroom, and Jessica made her way to the piano. Ever since Michael had joined the Junior Church staff, Jessica had decided "kiddy songs" weren't so bad after all.

Linda rolled her eyes. Jessica was being so obvious. Why couldn't Michael see that she was trying to trick him into marrying her? Surely he was smarter than that!

Oh, well, Linda thought. *I shouldn't even let it bother me. I have a chance to be in a real play, and here I am, worrying about Jessica and her silly competition.*

During dinner that afternoon, Linda told her family all about the play, and how much fun it was going to be. Mr. Lennard gave her permission to attend the tryouts on Tuesday, and Mrs. Lennard told her to tell Michael that she would be willing to help out with costumes or anything else he needed.

After the evening service, Linda joined the others in the singles classroom and eagerly waited to hear what Michael had to say. Quite a few people had gathered in the small room, and Mr. Donavan was there as well.

"Okay, everyone, thank you for your willingness to participate in our play," Michael said, standing up to face the group. "The play is called 'Behold, the Handmaid of the Lord', and the purpose of the play is to hopefully express Mary's willingness to submit to God's plan for her life. I believe God chose her to give birth to Jesus because He knew she was a humble and submissive woman and would be willing to say, 'Behold, the handmaid of the Lord. Be it unto me according to thy word.' I'm sure Mary was probably afraid of the idea of carrying God's Son in her womb, but she was willing to be used of God regardless of how she felt. I truly believe that if more of us were willing to say what Mary said, God would be able to use us in a much greater way."

Linda thought of her own recent struggle with submission, and how she had finally given in to the plan God had in store for her, whatever it may be. She was a little surprised at Michael's wisdom and insight.

"Pastor Grant has asked me to bring a short sermon following the play, and I will be speaking on that subject," Michael went on. "Now, as for the tryouts, those of you who would like to try for the part of either Mary or Joseph, please gather on the right side of the room. All of you who are interested in taking on minor roles may remain on the left."

Linda, Cathy, Becky, and Jessica, as well as three other girls, moved to the right side of the room. Ken Richardson and Jared Blake were among the five boys who gathered on the right side as well.

"Okay, I made copies of a short scene including both Mary and Joseph," Michael explained, handing them out to the group on the right. "You won't need to know the lines by heart, but it would be good to be familiar with the scene. On Tuesday, you will take turns rehearsing the scene for me, and I will then choose the best person for each part."

Michael then proceeded to select people from the remaining group to be shepherds, the angel, Gabriel, etc.

"Are there any questions?" Michael asked when he had finished.

"Is Joel Garber going to be Jesus?" Becky asked. "He's the newest baby."

"He's already six months old," Jessica objected.

"He's the closest we have," Michael said. "He'll do."

After Michael dismissed everyone, Linda headed down the hall, clutching her copy of the scene in which Mary tells Joseph about Gabriel's visit to her home. Obviously, it had been written by Michael as an added part to the story, and Linda was very much looking forward to reading it over.

"Linda, wait up."

Linda turned to see Cathy striding toward her. She was surprised to see that she was alone and not in her usual clique.

"Linda," Cathy said again when she had caught up with her. "I know you must really want the part of Mary. I mean, we all would. I just thought I should let you know what you're up against. You see, Jessica took drama in college. She can easily steal the part from all six of us other girls who are trying out. So, you can come and give it your best shot, but it would probably be less humiliating if you didn't bother. I would like the part as much as you would, but I think we both have to agree that Jessica deserves this part. Hey,...maybe you could be Elisabeth."

Linda just stared at her. "Why are you always trying to get rid of me?" she finally responded. "If I don't stand a chance, then why are you so worried about me being there?"

"I'm not worried," Cathy denied. "I just wanted to let you know what you're up against."

"Well, thank you," Linda said a little curtly. "I'll be sure to keep that in mind." Then she turned and walked briskly down the hall, fighting the tears that were threatening to escape.

"I don't understand," Linda told her father Tuesday morning. They had just arrived at the bookstore and were doing some overall straightening. "I've always felt like Cathy, Becky, and Jessica were one step ahead of me, but ever since Michael came back, they have been going out of their way to make sure I stay in the dust."

"It sounds to me like you make them feel insecure," Mr. Lennard observed.

"Me? Make *them* feel insecure?" Linda repeated. "How do you figure that?"

"Well, why else would they feel like they have to talk you down and get you out of their way?" Mr. Lennard asked. "They wouldn't even bother with you unless they saw you as a threat."

"Why would they see me as a threat?" Linda asked. "I don't even have anything they could be jealous of."

"You don't know that, Linda," Mr. Lennard said, gently. "Remember, a virtuous woman's price is far above rubies."

"I don't think I'm going to try out for the part of Mary tonight," Linda told him. "Cathy is right. If Jessica took drama in college, she would be much better at the part. She deserves it."

"I admire your self-sacrificing attitude, Linda, but don't give up this opportunity just because of what Cathy said. You deserve that part just as much as anyone else."

"Thanks, Dad, but I think I'd feel more comfortable playing a minor role anyway,"

Linda decided. "I'll just skip the tryouts and ask Michael for a different part."

Wednesday night, Linda weaved her way through the crowded church lobby in search of Michael. At least Cathy, Becky, and Jessica were nowhere in sight. She hoped they wouldn't be buzzing around Michael when she did finally find him.

She turned sideways and slipped between two people who were standing almost back-to-back. She was about ready to give up when she felt a tap on her shoulder. Turning around, she came face to face with Michael.

"Hey, Linda. I've been looking everywhere for you. How come you weren't at tryouts last night?"

"I...I decided I'd be more comfortable assuming a minor role," Linda explained hesitantly.

"I'm sorry to hear that," Michael told her, "because I've chosen you to play the part of Mary."

Chapter Ten

The Loser

"What...what do you mean?" Linda asked, looking both surprised and puzzled at the same time. "I didn't even try out. How do you know...?"

"Linda," Michael interrupted. "You don't need to try out for the part. Before I even scheduled the tryouts, I knew you would be the best choice. I just wanted to give everyone a fair chance, but it was just as I thought. You see, Linda, Mary is the ultimate example of submission. I believe she was very humble and selfless, and it is very important that those traits come out in her character. None of those other girls were able to capture that feel like you can. You have something they don't, Linda, and I need what you have for the play. Will you be Mary in my play?"

Linda just stared up at him, speechless. Never in her wildest dreams would she have ever even imagined that she would receive a personal invitation from Michael to assume the lead role in his Christmas play. It was almost as if he knew it had always been her dream to act.

Suddenly, Linda frowned. "Did...did my brother, Stephen, tell you that I've always wanted to act?"

"No," Michael said, looking pleased. "Have you?" he asked.

"Yes, I have," Linda replied. "I...I've never really told anyone before. I never thought I'd be given the opportunity to act."

She honestly couldn't believe she had just told Michael. His offer was so unexpected, she was having a hard time accepting the fact that it had been his own decision. Surely someone had suggested her as a choice!

"Are you sure I'm the one you want?" Linda asked, looking uncertainly into Michael's blue eyes.

Michael chuckled. "Linda, why is it so difficult for you to believe that you would be good for something? Of course I'm sure. I've been sure right from the start, but last night's tryouts confirmed it even more. So, what do you say?"

Linda grinned. "I'll do it!" she replied, exuberantly.

Thursday evening, at dinner, Linda found herself hardly able to stop talking about the play.

"I just can't believe Michael would pick me to play Mary when I wasn't even at the tryouts!" she mused. "I'm so excited. I can hardly wait."

"When's the first practice?" Amy asked.

Tomorrow evening at seven o' clock," Linda replied.

"I'm so glad you got the part, Honey," Mrs. Lennard said, smiling. "I can tell it means a lot to you."

"I'll help you study your lines if you help me study for this really big test I have tomorrow," Esther volunteered, balancing a few kernels of corn on her fork.

"Oh, Esther. Every test is a big test for you," Linda told her.

"That's because they're all really hard," Esther moaned.

"All right. I guess it's a deal," Linda said, chuckling.

"I wish I could be in a play," Jane said, wistfully.

Stephen helped himself to some more applesauce. "You can't even memorize two lines of poetry, Jane. How on earth would you memorize lines in a play?"

"Poetry is boring," Jane answered, making a face. "I could memorize lines for a play."

After helping with the dishes, Linda rushed outside to help Stephen with some last minute barn chores. The November air was crisp, and Linda could feel the wind stinging her face all the way to the barn. Once there, she hurried inside and slid the heavy door closed.

"Dad wants us to give all the animals extra hay tonight," Stephen said. "It's supposed to snow all night."

"So, I heard," Linda agreed.

"Where's Amy?" Stephen asked. "She was supposed to help too."

"She's coming," Linda assured him. "She has to help Jonah and Micah pick up the living room first."

"Those two sure keep everyone busy!" Stephen laughed.

Linda grinned, knowingly. Then she grew sober. "Steve, are you sure you didn't mention anything to Michael about my wanting to act?"

"Of course not," Stephen insisted. "I've only talked to the guy a couple of times. Besides, I promised I'd keep it a secret. Didn't I?"

"Yes, and I know you always keep your secrets," Linda responded. "I just can't believe Michael would choose me over all those other girls. It's like a dream come true."

Just then, the barn door slid open, and Amy hurried in, closing it quickly behind her. "It's freezing!" she exclaimed, shivering.

"Is it snowing yet?" Stephen asked.

"Not yet," Amy replied, "but it sure is cold enough. I hope we don't get snowed in, Linda. I wouldn't want you to miss your practice tomorrow night."

"I hope we don't either," Linda agreed. "I wouldn't want to miss it for the world."

Friday night, only a couple inches of snow covered the ground. Still, Linda guided the car cautiously down the somewhat slippery roads toward the church. She still couldn't believe she was actually on her way to her first practice. What would Cathy, Becky, and Jessica think about her landing the part of Mary? Would they be upset? Linda sincerely hoped not.

She pulled into the church parking lot fifteen minutes early. She had wanted to give herself enough time, so she wouldn't have to drive very fast on the snow covered streets. A few cars were already in the parking lot, so Linda decided she might as well go right on in.

Linda's footsteps hardly made a sound as she walked down the carpeted hall toward the side door of the auditorium. She could hear voices coming from inside, and as she drew closer, the voices became more and more distinct. She recognized one of the voices as Jessica's, and she sounded upset. Linda felt a feeling of dread fall over her. Was Jessica angry about losing the part of Mary?

Linda stopped at the door just in time to hear Cathy's voice, clear and distinct.

"We all think you've made a big mistake!" she said, decisively.

"Jessica took some drama classes in college," Becky's voice broke in. "Her performance of Mary was the best, and you know it!"

"That's right! Linda didn't even try out!" Jessica added. "How do you know she can even act?" Her voice sounded harsh and judgmental, even a little hurt.

"You're right," Michael's voice finally joined in. "I probably should have asked her to perform the scene for me, just to make sure."

"Of course you should have!" Becky snapped. "Linda probably tricked you into picking her for the part anyway. She couldn't care less that she would be stealing the part from someone much more qualified than herself."

"Unless you have some irrational feelings for her and just couldn't tell her no," Cathy accused.

"Look, I don't have any *irrational* feelings for Linda," Michael told them. He sounded a bit irritated. "I just think Linda would portray Mary the best."

"You have got to be kidding me," Jessica said. "Don't you know anything about Linda?"

"Look, Michael. Let us give you a little heads-up on what you're getting into with Linda Lennard." Cathy sounded as if she despised Linda's very name.

Linda leaned in closer to the door to be sure she could hear every word that would be said about her.

"For one thing, Linda is a complete loser," Cathy continued. "She submits like a two-year-old to her father's every whim."

"She can't even make decisions for herself," Jessica put in.

"She has no real job, no income, no place of her own, and she's never been trained in anything," Becky broke in.

"The question is, do you really want someone like 'Linda the loser' playing the main role in your Christmas play?" Cathy asked. "I mean, can you really trust someone with so little experience in anything to carry your entire play?"

"What if she completely ruined it?" Becky agreed.

"Personally, I wouldn't trust her to carry your play," Jessica warned him.

"Besides, she's just a dirty old farm girl," Becky noted. "Don't you want someone more sophisticated to play the part of Mary? Jessica actually possesses acting skills. Linda doesn't even carry herself like a professional. I mean, she lacks the kind of attitude and confidence that comes with acting."

There was a slight pause then, and Linda took the time to brush hot tears from her cheeks. She remained as close to the door as she could in order to hear how Michael would respond to all of this. How could he not agree? After all, most of it was true. Maybe Michael *was* wrong to choose her.

Suddenly, she silenced her thoughts as Michael finally spoke.

"Okay," he said, "maybe I was a bit hasty in making my decision. I admit that. But I don't see why you have to go and criticize her. There's nothing wrong with being willing to live at home and help out with the family business. In fact, I admire her loyalty and submission. It's hard to find those qualities in a person these days."

"Well, Michael, how noble of you to stick up for the lower class!" Cathy praised, lacing every word with relentless sarcasm, "but you can't deny the fact that Linda is not cut out for the part of Mary, and Jessica is."

"Face it, Michael," Becky pitched in. "As much as you may care for Linda, the only thing she'd be good for in this play is dusting the props."

Linda turned and rushed down the hall, tears streaming down her face. Bursting out the front door of the church, she ran straight for her car, climbed in, and headed back home. The part of Mary had suddenly lost it's thrill.

Chapter Eleven

A Humble Prayer

As she pulled into her own driveway, Linda was surprised she had been able to keep her composure long enough to get herself home safely. She stepped out of the car, closed the door, and ran for the barn —— the hay barn.

Dropping onto a bail of hay, Linda buried her face in her hands and burst into full-fledged tears. Never had she felt so defeated, so useless, so low and inferior. What else could they have said to make her feel any worse? Linda supposed they could have shoved her face-first into a puddle of mud, and she could have walked away feeling better than she did now.

How would Michael ever want to marry her now? At least he had stuck up for her, but now he knew she was good for nothing. He was even having second thoughts about using her in his play!

What am I thinking? Linda sobbed. *I don't even deserve Michael. He's an intelligent, good-looking, college-graduate with a bright future ahead of him. What would he want with a girl like me? I would be the only one gaining from that relationship. I can't expect Michael to give me everything he has when I have nothing to give him in return. Why did I ever even allow myself to wish such a thing?*

Just then, the barn door slid open. Linda looked up to see her mother hurry in and close the door against the cold air. She rushed to Linda then, arms outstretched, and enveloped her in a warm embrace.

"Linda!" she cried. "I thought I heard you pull up! I got worried when you didn't come inside. What happened?"

Linda wept into her mother's shoulder for quite some time before answering, and Mrs. Lennard waited patiently for her to gain control of her emotions enough to speak. Finally, her tears subsided, and Linda was able to recount to her mother the dismal conversation she happened to overhear.

"Oh, Mom!" she said when she had finished. "I wanted the part so much! I knew it was too good to be true that Michael would just hand it off to me!"

"Linda, when are you going to stop worrying about what other people think and just be yourself?" Mrs. Lennard asked, concern showing in her brown eyes. "God made you the way He wanted you to be, and He's willing to guide your life if you just let Him. It wasn't an accident that Michael asked you to play Mary, and it shouldn't matter to you what those other girls say or think. You should have just walked in there and practiced anyway. Then you could have proved to everyone that you were good for the part."

"I know, but I felt so bad after hearing all that they said. I couldn't bring myself to face them," Linda explained. "I just needed to get away. Besides, if Jessica is more qualified to play the part, I don't want to take it away from her."

"It's up to Michael," Mrs. Lennard said, firmly. "If he wants you to play the part, it doesn't matter how qualified Jessica is. Listen, Linda. Don't let those girls run your life. Don't let them decide what you should do, and how you should act, and what you're good for, and what you're not. Let God decide those things. He's in control, and He knows best. Maybe He wants you to have that part. Did you ever think about that?"

"No," Linda admitted. "I suppose if He does though, it won't matter how much Jessica wants the part."

"And it won't matter what she tries to say about you in order to talk Michael out of it," Mrs. Lennard added. "It won't work."

"I guess I'm just not very trusting, am I," Linda confessed.

"Well, you can start by forgetting everything that was said tonight," her mother told her. "If those girls think you're a loser, then they know nothing of what a Christian young lady ought to be. Now, why don't we go inside before we turn into ice cubes?"

Linda smiled as her mother stood up. "I was wondering when you would suggest that," she said, shivering.

Saturday morning, Linda helped her father straighten things up at the bookstore before opening time. The wall clock chimed nine o' clock, and Mr. Lennard turned the sign to say "OPEN". Just fifteen minutes later, the first customer walked in. Linda's heart skipped a beat. It was Michael!

Oh, no, Linda thought. *He's going to ask where I was last night! What will I tell him? Well, the truth of course. What else can I say?*

"Hello, Mr. Lennard. Hi, Linda. Did you just open?" Michael asked.

"Fifteen minutes ago," Mr. Lennard responded, cheerfully. "What can I do for you?"

Linda was about to shrink behind one of the shelves she was dusting when Michael said, "I was just wondering if you had a good book on the subject of prayer."

"I sure do," Mr. Lennard told him. "I think it's upstairs. I'll go check."

Mr. Lennard bounded up the stairs to the second floor, and then Michael walked over to Linda.

"Linda, I missed you last night at practice. I...I thought you said you were coming. Did you forget?"

"No, I came," Linda replied, avoiding eye contact with Michael. "I came, and...and then I left."

"Why did you leave?" Michael asked, frowning in puzzlement.

Linda turned away, bit her lip, and fought the tears that sprang into her eyes, willing them back. Then she took a deep breath and faced Michael again.

"I...I overheard what Cathy, Becky, and Jessica said about me. They were talking to you in the auditorium when I came in, and I stopped to listen at the door." Linda took another deep breath before continuing. "Michael, I don't feel right taking on the role of Mary if Jessica is much more qualified. Please use her instead."

"Linda, you don't understand!" Michael said, quickly. "I don't want Jessica to play Mary. She may have some professional acting skills, but she just doesn't portray it the right way. I thought I explained that to you on Wednesday. Now, I admit it wasn't quite fair to the others that I chose you before seeing you perform, but they had absolutely no right to say the things they said about you. I'm sorry you had to hear that."

"I'm not," Linda told him. "I've already heard it all before. I'm sorry *you* had to hear it. Now you know what a loser I really am." Then she stopped. What was she saying?

"Linda, you are not a loser!" Michael said emphatically. "Regardless of what you think, and regardless of what anyone says, you are not a loser. I heard about that little girl that was misbehaving in Junior Church. You took her out and talked to her, and she accepted Jesus Christ as her Saviour. What do you mean, you're a loser? You do a lot of good. How can you think that way about yourself?"

"Cathy, Becky, and Jessica have always had a way of making me feel that way about myself."

"They can't make you do anything!" Michael objected. "They may have more book knowledge than you, but you're smart where it counts. They don't know anything about being a Godly young lady, and I hope I'm not being too bold when I say it, but you would make a better wife than all three of them put together. They don't really even have a genuine desire to live for God. After all, that's the only thing that really counts in life. Linda, I wish you wouldn't call yourself a loser. You're going to make someone a great wife."

Linda lowered her head. "You don't know me very well if you think that," she told him. "I'm not good at anything. I mean, a guy wants someone who can be a help to him. He wants a wife who can be an asset to his life; someone who is smart enough to be of assistance when he needs something."

"Not me," Michael disagreed, shaking his head." Actually, my qualifications are much simpler than that. All I'm looking for in a wife is someone who has dedicated her life to God and is willing to serve Him right alongside me. Linda,…have you heard of the concept of Divine betrothal?"

"Yes," Linda replied. "Just recently."

"Do you believe in it?" he asked. Do you believe God chooses a mate for you and then plans for you to meet up and get married?"

Linda remained silent for a moment as if trying to decide if this were somehow a trick question.

"Well, yes," she finally replied.

"Then you believe that if you allow God to direct your life, He can give you a husband no matter how unqualified you feel, right?"

"Yes," Linda responded, weakly. She was beginning to see where Michael was going with this. Once again, she just wasn't trusting.

Just then, Mr. Lennard came running back down the stairs. "Here you go, Michael. I'm sorry it took so long. I didn't realize I hadn't put more on the shelf."

"Oh, that's all right, Mr. Lennard," Michael assured him. "Linda kept me company."

Mr. Lennard smiled approvingly as Linda blushed. Michael paid for the book and left, but his words stayed lodged in Linda's heart and mind.

Do you believe in Divine betrothal? Do you believe in Divine betrothal? Linda couldn't get those words out of her head. Did she believe in Divine betrothal? Did she truly believe that God would overlook her shortcomings and give her a husband anyway?

Later that night, Linda lay awake in bed. She tried to keep her eyes closed but no sleep came. Then she remembered something her father had once told her when she couldn't sleep.

"Try prayer, Linda," he had suggested. "That's what I do when I can't sleep. It relaxes the mind."

Linda thought about her conversation with Michael earlier that day, and suddenly the words came.

Lord Jesus, she prayed, silently. *You know my heart's desire is to be married, but I want your will in my life more than anything. If it's not part of your plan for me to be married, then please help me to accept that. But if you do want me to be married, please show me who the person is that you have chosen for me. Please work it all out in your time, and please help me to trust. In Jesus' name, Amen.*

Almost instantly, Linda felt a peace fill her soul, and within minutes she was sound asleep.

Chapter Twelve

Lost And Found

After leaving the Lennards' bookstore, Michael drove straight to his apartment and spent most of the day studying with his new book. Later that night, he tossed and turned in bed, unable to fall asleep. Frustrated, he climbed out of bed and went to get a glass of water. He still felt restless when he got back in bed. His mind seemed to be in full gear tonight and apparently had no intention of shutting down any time soon. Ironically, he was thinking about Linda. Lately, it seemed he hadn't been able to get her out of his mind. His thoughts wandered back to the day the church had celebrated his graduation and departure for college. Suddenly finding himself in the middle of a boring conversation about job-hunting, he had turned and noticed Linda standing behind the punch table. *Serving again as usual,* he had thought with an odd sense of admiration. He had always appreciated

Linda's quiet, faithful presence. As he broke from his group and approached the punch table, he wished there were some way he could express those feelings to her but no right words came.

"Hi, Linda," he'd said, reaching the table. "Well, I guess it's goodbye, actually. I'm going to miss everyone here, but I can't wait to see what takes place in these next few years. I mean, what if God calls me to preach while I'm studying the Bible?"

"What if He doesn't?" Linda had questioned.

"Well," Michael recalled himself answering, "I'm open to anything really. I want God to use me in whatever way He sees fit. I may come back from college and become a preacher, an assistant pastor, a Sunday School teacher, or just a faithful Christian who knows his Bible!" He had given her an exuberant smile, but he couldn't help noticing how quickly she had questioned him. Did she care that he was leaving? Did she…like him?

"How many years will you be going for?" Linda had asked him.

"Oh, four or five. I'm not sure yet."

"Don't you think that's…well… a long time to be away?"

"It's not that long. Besides, I'll be back for the summer each year. It'll go by fast." He had paused then. So she did care! "Well, I guess I'll be seeing you around. Next summer."

He had been trying to reassure her that they would see each other soon, but he had been wrong. How was he supposed to know his family would move to another state before he ever got a chance to see Linda again? He had thought about writing to her several times, but he didn't want to come across too bold. What if he had misinterpreted her, and she hadn't really liked him that much?

Michael lay in bed and thought about the first day he had come back to Courtland Baptist Church. He had been worried that Linda would have changed after so many years. How relieved he had been to find that she was still just as meek and quiet as ever! But he had also noticed a sadness in her eyes. At the time, he hadn't had a clue what it could be, but now he knew. She thought she was a loser. Cathy, Becky, and Jessica were mostly to blame for that. How could he help her realize how much she was really worth?

Suddenly, he stopped himself. Why did it mean so much to him to see Linda happy? Why was he finding himself thinking about her so much lately? Why did he have a nagging feeling that she just might be the one he should be marrying? Was it just his imagination, or did she care for him as well? How could he be sure? How could he know this was from God, and not just a childhood crush he had never grown out of? Then he knew. It was prayer of course. Prayer was the answer for all of life's problems.

Michael rolled out of his bed and knelt down beside it.

Dear Heavenly Father, he prayed, *I need some guidance, and I don't know of a better place to get it than from you. You know I've always liked Linda, and you know she is trying her best to serve you. I've never met a young lady who was as sincere, genuine, and devoted as Linda, but I don't know if she's meant for me or for someone else. Please show me clearly if she's the girl you have chosen for me or not.* He paused a moment as an idea sprang to his mind. *Lord,* he continued, *If Linda is the girl you want me to marry, please use a sermon to speak to her heart and show her she is not a loser. In your name, Amen.*

Sunday night after the evening church service, Linda went to find Michael. She needed to make sure she knew what time they were meeting on Tuesday to practice for the upcoming play. Michael had finally convinced her that there would be no Mary unless she played the part. Ken Richardson had been given the part of Joseph, and Jared Blake had received the part of the innkeeper. Jessica had begrudgingly taken on the role of Elisabeth, and Joel Garber was elected to play baby Jesus.

When Linda finally found him, Michael was busy talking to one of the men. She stood politely off to one side until he had finished his conversation and the man had said goodbye. Then she approached him.

"Michael," she said. "What time are we meeting on Tuesday?"

"Six o'clock," Michael replied. "Oh, I needed to talk to you and your father, Linda."

"Right now?" Linda asked, looking somewhat puzzled.

"Yes, if that's possible."

"All right. I'll go find him."

"Meet me in our singles classroom, okay?"

"Okay."

Linda hurried to find her father. What on earth could Michael possibly want to talk to them about? And why would he want to go somewhere private? Was it important?

After finding her father, the two of them entered the singles classroom where Michael was already waiting. They sat down, and Michael immediately began, addressing Linda.

"Linda, I want to be completely honest with you. Your father and Pastor Grant already know about this meeting. I talked to them this morning, and they agreed with what I am about to tell you."

Linda glanced over at Mr. Lennard for a moment as Michael continued.

"Lately, I...I haven't been able to stop thinking about you. You're...a constant presence in my mind, and...well...I've finally realized that I care for you, Linda. I always have. It's just that I've always been afraid to do anything or say anything about it, because I didn't want to make a wrong choice.

"The other day when I asked you if you believed in Divine betrothal, it was because I do, and I wanted to be sure you did too. You see, Linda, I've been having this nagging feeling in the back of my mind that you're the one I'm supposed to marry. I'm just not sure. I'm not even sure if...if you care for me too."

Michael's honest confession was not at all what Linda had been expecting to hear, but she was almost amazed to find that she didn't feel at all surprised or nervous. Something about his open frankness made her feel at ease. She looked up into his searching eyes and realized that his last sentence had been more a question than a statement. She then decided she owed him an honest confession as well.

"Michael, I've always liked you too. More than you'll ever know. I never could have even imagined that you liked me back."

"Yeah, well, I didn't really have a very good way of showing it, did I?" Michael said, chuckling. "Anyway, Linda, I said a prayer last night that I hope you will agree with."

"What is it?" Linda asked, eagerly.

"I asked God that if you were the right girl for me, He would use a sermon to speak to your heart and show you once and for all that you're not a loser."

Linda lowered her eyes. "Michael, I try hard not to think about it, and I try to tell myself I'm not, but everything seems to prove otherwise."

"Well, God can prove you're not," Michael said with determination. "Linda, will you pray with me about this?"

Linda slowly nodded her head. "Yes," she promised.

"And will you trust that God will do this if it's His will that we be together?"

"Yes," Linda said again as they all stood.

"I'll be praying as well," Mr. Lennard told him, shaking Michael's hand. "If God wills it, I'd be proud to have you as my son-in-law."

Linda's emotions practically went haywire over the next few weeks. Should she allow herself to get excited, or should she prepare herself for a possible disappointment? Would God really show her that she wasn't a loser when everything about her life contradicted it? Would she know for sure when He did?

Not only were Linda's thoughts filled with Michael and his proposal, but also the fact that the days before the Christmas play performance were quickly running out. The closer it got, the more anxious and excited Linda felt.

A week before the scheduled performance date, Michael held a cast party for all those involved in the play. The evening had included refreshments, fellowship, a few games, and a special thanks made by Michael himself for all those who had agreed to participate.

"Honestly, this upcoming play never would have been possible without all of your cooperation and hard work," Michael said. "Thank you so much. And now, Pastor Grant has agreed to bring us a little devotion from God's Word to end the evening. Pastor Grant?"

"Thank you, Michael. I appreciate this as well. We've never had a play performance at this church before, and I'm very much looking forward to seeing it. This Saturday evening though, I would like to talk to you about something that I hope will encourage all of you to do your very best at this play. I want to talk to you about losing your life for Christ's sake."

Linda felt her heart thump against her chest as it quickened its pace. This was it! Even before Pastor Grant delved into his devotion, Linda somehow knew this was the message she and Michael had been praying for. She hardly dared look over at Michael, but when she finally brought herself to do so, he was already looking at her. He knew too! This was their answer. Their answer was yes!

Her heart beating rapidly, Linda listened intently as Pastor Grant went on to talk about those who seek to find their life will end up losing it.

"God wants to work with a clean slate. He can't use you if you're already using yourself. God asks us Christians to lose our lives for His sake. That means to give up everything for God. Your dreams, your career, your goals in life. Are you willing to give all that up if God has other plans for you?

"All our lives we hear about climbing the ladder of success, or pursuing your dreams, or becoming good at one thing or another. Those all sound like good things, but God asks us to give them up for His sake. In return, He promises to reward us. Therefore, in losing our life we actually find it. Matthew 10:39 says, 'He that findeth his life shall lose it: and he that loseth his life for my sake shall find it.' I guess according to Jesus, it's actually the losers that come out on top. God will reward you and give you a life you never could have found on your own.　Young people, lose your life for Christ's sake and He will reward you; maybe even by showing you just the right person to marry."

Linda and Michael exchanged knowing grins. Linda felt as if they were school-aged children sharing a well-kept secret. After all, they were the only two in the entire room who knew how much this particular message meant to them. Linda had never thought about that verse and how it applied to her life. God wanted her to lose her life so she could find it, and now she had.

The following Sunday, Courtland Baptist Church's singles class performed their Christmas play without a hitch. Even baby Joel seemed to cooperate. It was just four days before Christmas. After the play, Michael preached his sermon about Mary and her wonderful example of submission.

When he finished, he announced, "I want to thank everyone for being here tonight. I also want to thank everyone who participated in the performance of this play, but I especially want to thank Linda Lennard for her excellent portrayal of Mary. Linda, would you please come up here?"

Linda frowned and felt her heart flutter. Why was Michael drawing so much attention to her? She blushed and walked up to the platform next to Michael.

"Linda is the best example of submission I've ever seen in a young lady, and I think she made a great Mary. But I also think she will make a great wife." Linda blushed even deeper as Michael continued. "Aside from her wonderful acting job, there are many other reasons why I'm going to do what I'm about to do tonight."

Michael turned to face Linda. "Linda Lennard, will you marry me?"

Linda was speechless for a moment. She had known it was coming, but she hadn't known he would do it like this. She looked out at the waiting crowd and noticed Cathy, Becky, and Jessica looking completely defeated. So much for their competition. God had had other plans.

Linda turned back to Michael and smiled. "Yes, I will!" she replied.

After the service, Michael and Linda stood together in the lobby as people walked by and congratulated them. The ladies poured over the beautiful diamond ring Michael had given Linda, and excitedly volunteered to help with her wedding plans.

After the crowd had died down, Linda was surprised to see Jessica slowly make her way up to her.

"Linda, I…I just wanted to tell you that I was wrong about you. After what Pastor Grant said about losing your life for Christ's sake, I realized that you were on the right track after all. I just want you to know that…well…I'm happy for you. You got exactly what you deserved. I hope you'll forgive me for the way I treated you."

Linda looked surprised. "Of course I will," she said, giving her a hug. "And…and thank you."

Only three months later, Michael and Linda were married. It was hard to believe that just a few months earlier, Linda had given up all hope that she would ever amount to anything, and now she had become Michael's wife. God had been in control the entire time, and Linda had learned a valuable lesson. Losers are winners in God's Book because, if you lose your life for Christ's sake, you *will* find it.